Walt Disney's
WINNIE THE POOH
STORYBOOK

Walt Disney's

WINNIE THE POOH

STORYBOOK

Edited by Darlene Geis

Harry N. Abrams, Inc., *Publishers*, New York

Project Director: Darlene Geis
Designer: Dirk Luykx

Library of Congress Cataloging-in-Publication Data
Walt Disney's Winnie the Pooh storybook/edited by Darlene Geis.
p. cm.
Summary: Four episodes in the adventures of Winnie the Pooh and
his friends, based on the four cartoons made by Walt Disney.
ISBN 0–8109–1129–9
[1. Toys—Fiction.]   I. Geis, Darlene.   II. Milne, A. A. (Alan
Alexander), 1882–1956. Winnie the Pooh.   III. Walt Disney
Productions.   IV. Title: Winnie the Pooh storybook.
PZ7.W72989 1989
[E]—dc19   88–24118

Copyright © 1989 The Walt Disney Company

"Winnie the Pooh." Words and music by Richard M. Sherman and
Robert B. Sherman. © 1963 Wonderland Music Company, Inc.

A Times Mirror Company

Printed and bound in Japan

CONTENTS

Song: Winnie the Pooh   6

Winnie the Pooh and the Honey Tree   9

Winnie the Pooh and the Blustery Day   31

Winnie the Pooh and Tigger Too   63

Winnie the Pooh and a Day for Eeyore   99

WINNIE THE POOH

Words and Music By
RICHARD M. SHERMAN
and ROBERT B. SHERMAN

Win - nie The Pooh, Win - nie The Pooh, Tub - by lit - tle cub - by all stuffed with fluff. He's Win - nie The Pooh, Win - nie The Pooh. Wil - ly nil - ly sil - ly ole bear. ____ Deep in the hun - dred ac - re wood Where Chris - to - pher Ro - bin plays, ____ You will find the en-

WINNIE THE POOH AND THE HONEY TREE

Once upon a time, a long time ago, about last Thursday, Winnie the Pooh lived in an enchanted forest, all by himself, under the name of "Sanders." (Which means that he had the name over the door in gold letters, and he lived under it.)

One day when he heard his Pooh-coo clock go "Pooh, coo. Pooh, coo. Pooh, coo," he knew it was time for something. But as he was a Bear of Very Little Brain, he didn't know quite what. He stood in front of his mirror and thought in the most thoughtful way he could think.

"I haven't thought of anything, have you?" he asked the Pooh Bear in the mirror. The Pooh Bear shook its head.

"No, neither have I."

"Think, think, think," said Pooh to himself. "Oh, yes! It's time for my stoutness exercises."

And Pooh began to sing his Stoutness Song. He reached up and bent down, touching his toes and groaning as he sang. And to make his exercise time pass more pleasantly he thought of cheerful things like honey, bread and butter, chocolate candy, and ice cream.

By the time Pooh finished his stoutness exercises he had worked up quite an appetite, and felt the need of a little something to eat. He climbed up on a chair to reach a honey jar down from the top shelf of his pantry. It was almost empty and Pooh had to stick his head way inside the jar, licking at the very bottom.

"Oh, bother," he complained. "Empty again. Only the sticky parts left," and he struggled so hard to get the last drop that he fell off the chair with the jar stuck over his face.

At that moment a bee flew in the open window and buzzed around the jar, landing on Pooh's right ear.

"That buzzing noise means something," said Pooh as he pulled his head free of the jar. "And the only reason for making a buzzing noise that I know of is because you're a bee."

Pooh watched the bee fly out the window. "And the only reason for being a bee," he said as he watched the bee fly toward the top of a nearby tree, "is to make honey.

"And the only reason for making honey," he added, licking the last of the honey from his sticky paws, "is so I can eat it! Ha, ha, ha!"

So Winnie the Pooh followed the bee and climbed up the honey tree. He climbed and he climbed and he climbed, and as he climbed he hummed a hungry little hum.

Pooh shinnied up the tree, hit his head on a branch, and climbed up to the next limb. He continued climbing and singing as he watched the bee fly into a hole above him.

Pooh carefully moved higher, onto a slender branch that bent under his weight till it almost touched the large hole in the tree. He tried to reach into the hole but at that moment the branch broke and he fell, banging his head and his bottom on the other branches on the way down.

"Oh, help!" Pooh cried out. "If only I hadn't . . . You see, what I meant to dooo," he explained as he crashed from branch to branch.

"Oh, dear," he groaned as he scraped past the last six branches. "This all comes, I suppose, from liking honey so much."

At that Pooh took one last somersault, and flew gracefully into a prickly gorse-bush. "Oh, bother!" he exclaimed, as he crawled out of the gorse-bush, brushed the prickles from his nose, and began to think again.

And who do you suppose was the first person he thought of? It was Christopher Robin.

11

Now, Christopher Robin lived in a big tree in another part of the forest where he could be near his friends, Eeyore, Owl, Kanga and baby Roo, and Piglet, and help them with their problems.

The old gray donkey, Eeyore, kept losing his tail and Christopher Robin had to nail it back on again. Kanga, Roo, and Owl gave their advice about where to put it.

"No matter," said Eeyore. "Most likely I'll lose it again, anyway."

Christopher patted the sad-looking donkey.

"Cheer up, Eeyore. Don't be so gloomy. Try swishing it," he said after nailing it on again.

Eeyore swished his tail, looking between his legs to see if it worked. "Thanks. It's not much of a tail but I'm sort of attached to it."

Just then, along came Winnie the Pooh, calling out a cheerful "Good morning!"

"Oh, good morning, Winnie the Pooh," said Christopher. "Good morning, Pooh Bear," chorused Owl, Kanga, and Roo.

"If it is a good morning, which I doubt," added Eeyore.

Christopher was glad to see his bear, and off the two of them went to the house in the big tree. "What are you looking for, Pooh Bear?" Christopher asked.

Pooh had stopped in front of a tricycle with a blue balloon tied to its handlebars. "I just said to myself, coming along, thinking and wondering if you had such a thing as, oh . . . such a thing, Christopher, ah . . . as a balloon about you?"

"What do you want a balloon for?"

Pooh looked around to be sure no one could hear, and then he whispered, "Honey!"

"But you don't get honey with a balloon," said Christopher, untying the balloon and handing the string to Pooh. The balloon started to fly upward.

"I do," said Pooh, as he was lifted off the ground.

"How?" Christopher asked.

"I shall fly like a bee, up to the honey tree, see?"

Christopher pulled Pooh back down to the ground. "But just a minute, Pooh. You can't fool bees that way."

"You'll see," Pooh said with a wise look. "Now, would you be so kind, Christopher Robin, as to tow me to a very muddy place that I know of?"

So Christopher Robin very kindly towed Pooh to the muddy place where Pooh rolled and rolled until he was black all over.

"There, now," he said. "Isn't this a clever disguise?"

"What are you supposed to be?" Christopher asked.

"Why, a little black rain cloud, of course. With the blue balloon above me, the bees will think I am part of the sky, just a small black rain cloud. That will deceive them."

"Silly old Bear," Christopher smiled at him affectionately. But he aimed Pooh and his balloon at the honey tree and stood below watching as the bear sang a little rain-cloud song to fool the bees.

As he floated closer to the hole in the honey tree, Pooh continued his singing, and then, when a little gust of wind blew him closer to the tree, Pooh stuck his hand into the hole full of honey and pulled it out all dripping and sticky. A bee flew over and settled on his nose.

Pooh continued to sing bravely. He was getting nervous about the bee's attentions. "Christopher Robin!" he called down in a loud whisper. "I think the bees S·U·S·P·E·C·T something."

"Perhaps they think you're after their honey."

"It may be that. You never can tell with bees."

More bees were flying out of the hole in the tree, circling the little black rain cloud and making him extremely uncomfortable.

"Christopher Robin!" he called down. "I think it would help with the deception if you would open your umbrella and say, 'Tut, tut, it looks like rain.'"

Well, Christopher Robin laughed to himself and said, "Silly old Bear," but he went to get his umbrella, because he was so fond of Pooh. When he returned he walked back and forth with his big black umbrella over his head and said, "Tut, tut, it looks like rain."

Meanwhile, the bees were flying closer and closer to Winnie the Pooh, settling on his paw smeared with honey and buzzing angrily. One bee thought the sight of a bear hanging from a balloon with a lot of bees buzzing around him was so funny that he lay back on a branch and laughed and laughed.

Pooh, worried, called down to Christopher Robin, "Christopher Robin! *I have come to a very important decision. These are the wrong sort of bees.*"

Suddenly the balloon broke loose from its string and Pooh barely had a chance to catch hold of it. A swarm of bees chased the balloon as it swirled about with Pooh hanging on for dear life.

"Christopher Robin!" he called, as the air suddenly went out of the balloon. "Oh, bother, I think I shall come down."

"I'll catch you," said Christopher, and he did. Pooh's arms were so

stiff from hanging onto the balloon's string all that time that they stayed
straight up in the air for three hours.

With the angry bees swarming after them, Christopher picked up
Pooh and jumped into the mudhole with him. Opening his big black
umbrella, he sheltered them both.

"Christopher Robin," said Pooh solemnly, his arms still stiffly
raised, "you never can tell with bees."

Now Pooh was not the sort to give up easily. After he left
Christopher Robin he was walking along with his mind still on honey,
and he stuck to it. First he thought, "Honey rhymes with bunny, and
bunny rhymes with—ah—Rabbit!" And there in front of him was Rabbit's house, a snug little burrow in the side of a hill.

Pooh stood close to the entrance and said loudly, "I like Rabbit because he uses short easy words like 'How about lunch?' and 'Help yourself, Pooh.'"

Inside his house, Rabbit heard his unexpected visitor and scurried to clear the food off of the table. "Pooh? Lunch? Oh, no, not again! Oh, my goodness gracious," he muttered to himself.

"Is anybody at home?" Pooh called. "What I said was, 'Is anybody at home?'"

"Nobody," Rabbit answered.

"Bother," said Pooh. "Somebody must be there," he added, bending down to call into the hole. "Because somebody must have said, 'Nobody.'"

Rabbit ran to the hole, looked out, saw Pooh, and quickly grabbed his honey jar from the table. Pooh called again, "Rabbit, isn't that you?"

"No," said Rabbit, talking into the honey jar and making a strange echoing sound.

"Well, isn't that Rabbit's voice?" Pooh asked.

"I don't think so," said Rabbit. "It isn't meant to be."

Pooh stuck his head into the hole and looked around. "Hello, Rabbit," he said.

"Oh, hello, Pooh Bear!" Rabbit tried to sound surprised. "Oh, Pooh Bear, what a pleasant surprise! Ah, how about a mouthful of something?"

Pooh squeezed through the hole and came into Rabbit's cozy little house. There was a round table with a checked tablecloth all set for lunch. Pooh tied the napkin around his neck, picked up the spoon, and started to hum a happy little hum of anticipation.

"Would you like condensed milk or honey on your bread?" Rabbit asked. Pooh was so excited that he said, "Both." Then, so as not to seem greedy, he added, "But never mind the bread. Just a small helping, if you please."

Rabbit poured a small amount of honey on the plate and Pooh looked at it with undisguised disappointment. "Well, I did mean a little *larger* small helping," he said, looking hungrily at the jar.

"Perhaps it would save time if you took the whole jar," Rabbit told him, resigned to seeing the last of his honey.

So Pooh ate and ate and ate and ate and ate and ate and ate and ate and ATE until at last, his stomach blown up like a balloon, he put down the empty honey jar and said, in a rather sticky voice, "I must be going now. Good-bye, Rabbit." He shook Rabbit lovingly by the paw, leaving him sticky too.

"Well, good-bye," said Rabbit, "if you're sure you won't have any more."

Pooh turned at the door. "Is there any more?"

"No, there isn't, not really."

"I thought not," said Pooh and he eased himself into Rabbit's front door. He pulled with his front paws and he pushed with his hind legs and in a little while his nose was outside . . . and then his ears . . . then his front paws . . . then his shoulders . . . and then, "Oh, help," said Pooh, and he tried to go back. "Oh, bother!" said Pooh. "I shall have to go on. Oh, help *and* bother! I can't do either!"

Now by this time Rabbit was ready to go for a walk but when he found his front door full, he gave Pooh a push. "Oh, dear. Oh, gracious. This all comes from eating too much," he said sternly.

"It all comes from not having front doors big enough," Pooh answered crossly.

Rabbit pushed and pushed at Pooh's back, trying to get him out of the hole, but Pooh couldn't budge.

"There's only one thing to do," Rabbit muttered. "I'll fetch Christopher Robin." And out the back door he ran, hopping past Pooh, stuck in the front door.

Owl flew down from his branch and looked at Pooh. "Who, who, who," he said. "Well, if it isn't Pooh Bear. Splendid day to be up and about one's business, quite. Ha, ha, ha. Oh, I say, are you stuck?"

"Hello, Owl. Not stuck, just resting and thinking and, ah, humming to myself. Hum, hum, hum, hum."

Owl cleared his throat for an important pronouncement. "You, sir, are stuck. A wedged bear in a great tightness," he said sternly. "In a word, irremovable. Ha, ha, ha. Now, obviously this situation calls for an expert."

At that moment Owl was knocked over by Gopher, who popped up from his tunnel right under Owl's feet.

"Somebody call for an excavation expert?" Gopher asked. "I'm at your service. What's your problem?"

"It seems," said Owl, dusting himself off, "the entrance to Rabbit's domicile is impassable. To be exact, plugged."

"And you want me to dig it out?" Gopher inspected Rabbit's front door carefully. "Uh, the first thing to be done is to get rid of that bear. He's gummin' up the whole project."

"Dash it all," said Owl. "He *is* the project."

While Pooh rested patiently Gopher climbed up on him and started to dig with his strong little paws. The dirt fell on Pooh, and Gopher stopped to dust him off. "Mighty hard diggin'," he told the bear. "Big job. Take two or three days."

"Three days?" Pooh groaned. "What about lunches?" he asked, now quite alarmed.

"No problem," Gopher told him. "I always go home for lunch.

Think it over and let me know," he said and disappeared down his hole.

Pooh was beginning to despair when Rabbit's welcome voice called, "Here we come. Don't worry!" And there, indeed, were Rabbit and Christopher Robin, hurrying toward him.

"Cheer up, Pooh Bear," Christopher called. "We're coming. We'll get you out." But Eeyore, munching some grass nearby, added, "Well, maybe."

When Christopher saw the front half of Pooh he said, "Silly old Bear," in such a loving voice that they all felt quite hopeful. Pooh had begun to think Rabbit might never be able to use his front door again, and that would have been awful.

"Here, give me your arm," Christopher said, "and Rabbit and I will pull together."

They strained and they pulled, but Pooh didn't budge.

"Well, if we can't pull you out, Pooh, perhaps we can push you back," Christopher said.

Rabbit scratched his whiskers and pointed out that once Pooh was pushed back into his front room, though no one was happier to entertain Pooh than he was, well, people lived in different kinds of houses, some in trees, some in the ground, and it took some getting used to.

"You mean I'd never get out?" asked Pooh.

"Well, I mean having got this far it seems a pity to waste it."

Christopher nodded. "There's only one thing we can do. Wait for you to get thin again."

"Oh, bother," said Pooh. "How long will that take?"

Eeyore's gloomy voice answered, "Days, weeks, months, who knows?"

They all settled down to wait as patiently as possible for Pooh to get slim again. Rabbit's front room was rather unattractively decorated with the south end of Pooh, and Rabbit asked Pooh if he could fix it up a bit. He found a frame to frame it with, some antlers, and a little shelf, and then he tickled Pooh by painting a moose face on his back end to go with the antlers. Rabbit was quite pleased with the effect.

Kanga and Roo came by one day to cheer up their friend. "Pooh, Roo has a little surprise for you." Roo held out a bouquet and said, "Flowers."

"Honeysuckle," said Pooh. And he began to eat them.

"No, Pooh, you don't eat them, you *smell* them!" Kanga said.

While Pooh's south end was stuck in Rabbit's house, his north end was stuck outdoors, both waiting for Pooh's middle to get thin again. Day after day, night after lonely night they waited. Christopher held an umbrella over the brave bear when it rained; the Gopher came to have a midnight lunch when he was on the night shift once, but that was no fun for poor hungry Pooh.

And then, one morning when Rabbit was beginning to think that he might never be able to use his front door again, it happened. Rabbit leaned against Pooh's south end, and it budged. He was so excited, he ran out of his back door and around to the front to tell Pooh the news.

Then off to Christopher Robin he hopped.

"He budged! Hooray! Christopher . . . uh . . . oh, Christopher Robin! He budged!"

Rabbit called to all the others, "Today is the day!"

Kanga and Roo and Eeyore and Owl and Piglet joined him in a happy song, while Christopher beat his drum and all the animals marched to Rabbit's front door. Then, as though they were playing a game of tug-of-war, they all got in line behind Christopher Robin and pulled and pulled at Pooh's arms. He began to move. With one last mighty heave and ho, Christopher and his friends gave Pooh's paws a powerful pull, while inside the house Rabbit gave his back a powerful push.

Like a cork popping out of a bottle, Pooh shot out of the hole. He flew over the treetops through the air, straight into the hole in the honey tree.

The bees swarmed out in surprise, while Pooh lapped up their honey.

"Don't worry, Pooh. We'll get you out!" Christopher called.

"No hurry. Take your time," Pooh answered in a sticky, happy voice, high up in the honey tree.

"Yum, yum. Bears love honey, and I'm a Pooh Bear. Yum, yum. Time for something sweet."

WINNIE THE POOH AND THE BLUSTERY DAY

On a blustery day, when the wind was blowing and the trees were swaying, Winnie the Pooh decided to take a stroll and perhaps visit his Thoughtful Spot where he could sit and think. On the way, he made up a little hum about the weather, describing the wind and the trees and the leaves on this blustery day. Luckily, Pooh's Thoughtful Spot was in a sheltered place, and when he got there he sat down and thought very very hard.

Gopher popped out of a nearby hole. "What's wrong? Got a headache?"

"No," said Pooh. "I was just thinking."

"Well, if I was you, I'd think about skedaddlin' out of here, with all this weather."

"Why?" said Pooh.

"Because it's Windsday!" Gopher laughed and popped back into the hole.

"Windsday," Pooh said to himself. "I think I shall wish everyone a happy Windsday today, and I shall begin with my very dear friend Piglet.

Now, Piglet lived in a very grand house in the middle of a beech tree in the middle of the forest—and Piglet loved it. The house had been in the family for a long long time and had his grandfather's name on a broken sign to prove it: TRESPASSERS WILL.

"That," Piglet would explain, "is short for TRESPASSERS WILLIAM, my grandfather's name."

This blustery day little Piglet was out sweeping leaves from the path in front of his house when the wind blew him right into Pooh.

"Happy Windsday, Piglet," said Pooh, catching at Piglet as another gust of wind blew him right off his feet and up into the air.

"Where are you going, Piglet?" Pooh called as he rushed after him.

"That's what I'm asking myself," Piglet answered as the wind tossed him around. "Where? Whoops!"

Pooh grabbed at Piglet's scarf, which started to unravel. There was Pooh, holding the end of a piece of yarn while the rest of the scarf unravelled into a long kite string—with Piglet flying high as a kite at the other end of it.

"Hang on tight, Piglet!" Pooh called, trying to keep up with the Piglet kite. The wind carried it over Kanga's house where Roo popped up out of his mother's pouch, crying excitedly, "A kite!"

"Oh, my goodness!" Kanga exclaimed. "It's Piglet!"

Pooh, holding on to the other end of the string, was pulled right past Kanga and Roo.

"Happy Windsday!" he called to them as he went by.

Roo clapped his hands with delight. "Can I fly Piglet next, Pooh?" he squeaked.

The terrified Piglet, tossing in the wind, could only say, "Oh, dear. Oh, de-de-de-de-dear."

Over the Hundred Acre Wood the Piglet kite flew, with Pooh following on the ground, faithfully clutching his end of the string.

Eeyore had just placed the last board on a lean-to he was building. "There," he said with some satisfaction. "That should stand against anything."

At that moment, Piglet, flying through the air, still holding onto the string from his scarf, called out in a small squeak, "Oh, oh, help! Help! Somebody save me!" as he flew over Eeyore's new lean-to. But Pooh, at the other end of the string on the ground, was pulled right through the lean-to, completely destroying it. Eeyore watched in dismay as the boards he had just built up came tumbling down.

"Happy Windsday, Eeyore," Pooh called to him as he swept by.

"Thanks for noticing me," Eeyore answered glumly.

The wind carried Piglet over Rabbit's vegetable garden where Rabbit was admiring the neat rows of carrots that were almost ready for harvesting. Pooh, still hanging onto the string for dear life, was pulled bouncing along the ground.

He dug his feet into the dirt and just had time to call out, "Happy Windsday, Rabbit!" when he was yanked right into the carrot patch.

"Pooh Bear!" Rabbit shouted. "Stop! Oh, go back! Oh, no!" For the helpless Pooh was digging up Rabbit's rows of carrots with his feet as he was pulled along by the string. The carrots flew through the air and piled up in a tall stack in Rabbit's wheelbarrow.

"Next time I hope he blows right through my rutabaga patch," Rabbit said, grateful for the unexpected help with his harvesting.

The wind was now blowing so strongly that Pooh was lifted right off the ground and flew along with Piglet. Into the Hundred Acre Wood the two friends were carried, smack bang onto Owl's tree house.

Owl had been sitting, snug in his rocking chair, half awake and half asleep, when he heard Piglet squeak, "Whoops!"

"Who, who, who, who is it?" Owl was startled. Then he saw Piglet outside, blown flat against his window.

"Well, I say now. Someone has pasted Piglet on my window," Owl exclaimed. At that there was a bump on the window and Pooh's voice gasping, "Ooh."

"Well, well," Owl laughed. "Pooh, too. This is a surprise."

Owl opened the top half of his door and Pooh and Piglet were blown in and plastered flat against the wall. As soon as Owl closed the door and shut the wind out Pooh and Piglet dropped from the wall onto a chair and a stool.

"Well," said Owl. "Am I correct in assuming it is a rather blustery day outside?"

"Oh, yes," Pooh agreed. "That reminds me, a happy Windsday, Owl."

The wind was blowing harder than ever and Owl's house was swaying back and forth, as trees will in a storm. The table and chair and stool slid across the floor, first one way, then another, and a dish, a cup, a spoon, and a large jar on the table skated back and forth across its top. The spoon flipped out of the cup and hit Piglet in the head. Pooh, watching the jar intently, asked Owl, "Is there honey in that pot?"

"Oh, yes, yes, of course. Help yourself. Now, as I was saying, this is a mild spring zephyr compared to the big wind of '67 . . ."

Pooh took the lid off the honey jar, and eagerly dug his paw into the honey. All the while, he and a thoroughly frightened Piglet, the table, and the chairs were sliding back and forth each time the tree house rocked. Owl, paying no attention, calmly went on with one of his endless stories. ". . . or was it '76? Oh, well, I remember the big blow very well."

"I'll remember this one, too," said Piglet who, being small, was banged about a good deal more than the others.

Owl continued, "It was the year my Aunt Clara went to visit her cousin who was not only gifted on the glockenspiel but, being a screech owl, also sang soprano in the London Opera."

Pooh and Piglet meanwhile were being rocked from one side of the house to the other and Piglet, who just managed to grab the honey pot as it was sliding off the table, on the next jolt was thrown upward and rammed it over Pooh's nose.

"Thank you, Piglet," came Pooh's muffled voice.

"Her constant practicing," Owl droned on, "so unnerved my aunt—" At that moment the dish cupboard fell on Owl with a great clatter of crockery.

"She laid a seagull egg by mistake. Whoo!"

And then the tree, with Owl's house in it, fell to the ground with a terrible crash.

Owl straightened his feathers and peered out the window, which now lay on the forest floor.

"Well, I say now, someone has . . . Pooh, did you do that?"

As soon as Christopher Robin heard of the disaster he, Rabbit, and Eeyore hurried to the scene of Owl's misfortune. They found Owl rocking in his chair in front of the smashed tree house.

"What a pity, Owl," said Christopher, surveying the damage. "I don't think we will ever be able to fix it."

Eeyore looked at the fallen tree house. "If you ask me, when a house looks like that, it's time to find another one."

"That's a very good idea, Eeyore," said Christopher.

"Might take a day or two, but I'll find a new one for Owl," Eeyore offered.

"Good." Owl settled himself more comfortably in his rocking

chair. "That will just give me time to tell you about my Uncle Clyde, a very independent barn owl. He became enamored of a pussycat and went to sea in a pea-green boat."

As Owl talked on and on and on, the blustery day turned into a blustery night, and everyone returned to his own comfortable house.

To Pooh it was a very anxious sort of night, filled with anxious sorts of noises. And one of the noises was a sound that had never been heard in the Hundred Acre Wood before.

"Rrrrrrr."

Pooh slid under the covers with just enough room for his eyes to look around.

"Rrrrrrr."

"Ah, is that you, Piglet?" he asked in a quavery wavery voice.

"Rrrrrrr."

"Well, tell me about it tomorrow, Eeyore," said Pooh in a hopeful voice.

"Rrrrrrr."

"Uh, come in, Christopher Robin," said Pooh from under the covers.

The front door with the bar across it began to rattle. Pooh got out of bed, picked up his popgun, and being a Bear of Very Little Brain, decided to invite the new sound in.

He marched to the door, opened it, and looked out into the darkness. In a trembling voice he called, "Hello, out there. I hope nobody answers."

There was a sudden flash of stripes.

"Rrrrrrr! Hello, I'm Tigger!" And Pooh found himself on the floor with Tigger's feet on his chest.

"Oh! Oh, you scared me!" Pooh stammered, looking up into a strange striped face with whiskers.

Tigger laughed. "Oh, sure I did. Everyone's scared of Tigger. Who are you?"

"I'm Pooh," said Pooh as well as he was able with Tigger's feet on his chest.

"Ah, Pooh," Tigger chuckled. Then he pushed Pooh's nose in with his nose and looked directly into his eyes. "What's a Pooh?"

"You're sitting on one," Pooh said in a breathless sort of voice.

"I am? Oh, well, glad to meet you. Name's Tigger," and Tigger climbed off of Pooh and shook his hand. "T-I-double grrr. That spells Tigger."

"But what *is* a Tigger?" Pooh demanded.

At that Tigger broke into a little dance. "You asked for it," he laughed, and in a loud voice he sang his very own braggy song about how wonderful Tiggers were. He bounced around on his springy legs and bottom, having so much fun showing off that in spite of himself Pooh was amused. Tigger finished his song proudly proclaiming that, best of all, he was the one and only Tigger. There were no others like him in the world.

Pooh pointed to his mirror standing against the wall. There was a big Tigger reflected in it. "Then what's that over there?" he asked.

Tigger turned and looked at the mirror. "Hey, look! Look!" he exclaimed. "What a strange-looking creature!" He walked up to examine it more closely. "Look at those beady little eyes. Hmm. And that pur-posti-rus chin." Then, standing right in front of the mirror, he laughed. "And those ricky-diculus striped pajamas!"

"Looks like another Tigger to me," said Pooh.

"Oh, no it's not," Tigger insisted. "I'm the only Tigger." And he turned and growled at the Tigger in the mirror, scared himself, and ran out of the room. But he was back in an instant.

"Watch me scare the stripes off of this impostor," he laughed. Once more Tigger growled "Rrrrr" at the mirror, scared himself again, and dived under the table, leaving only his tail out. "Pooh, is . . . is . . . is . . . ah, is he gone?"

"All except the tail," Pooh answered. Tigger pulled his tail under the table.

"He's gone. You can come out now, Tigger."

Tigger bounced out, knocked Pooh flat on his back, and stood on his stomach.

"Rrrrrr. Hello, I'm Tigger."

"You said that," Pooh told him with some annoyance.

"Ah, well," Tigger answered with his feet still on Pooh's chest. "Did I say I was hungry?"

"I don't think so."

"Well, there, I'll say it. *I am hungry.*" And he looked right at the honey pot on Pooh's table. Pooh said nervously, "Not for honey, I hope? What do Tiggers like?" At that Tigger jumped up and down for joy. "Honey! Oh, boy! Honey!" He sat down at Pooh's table, grabbed Pooh's honey pot, and dug in. "That's what Tiggers like the very best," he said as he scooped up a galopshus pawfull.

Pooh said sadly, "I was afraid of that."

Tigger smacked his lips. "Oh . . . yum . . ." he started to say. Then, when he really got a taste, he pushed the honey pot away and made an awful face. "Yuck!"

"But you said that's what Tiggers liked," Pooh began.

Tigger was trying to wipe off the honey. "That icky sticky stuff is only fit for Heffalumps," he said. "Or Woozles."

"You mean elephants and weasels," Pooh corrected him carefully.

"That's what I said, Heffalumps and Woozles," Tigger repeated.

"What do they do, these Hallalapps and Whichels? Uh, what do they do?" Pooh asked.

"Oh, nothing much. Just steal honey," Tigger said carelessly.

Pooh grabbed his honey pot. "Steal honey?" he asked.

"Yeah, they sure do," said Tigger. "Well, I'd better be bouncing along. Good night." And off he went into the forest singing his braggy song.

Well, Pooh thought, if what Tigger said was true, and there really

were Heffalumps and Woozles about, there was only one thing to do: Take Drastic Precautions to protect his precious honey.

So Pooh put a bar across his door, looked under the bed, took out his trusty popgun, and fit a cork into the barrel. Then he marched past his mirror, turned and rushed back to have a look at himself with his gun. "Oh, hello," he said to the Bear in the mirror. "Am I glad to see you! It's

more friendly with two. Now, you go that way and I'll go this way. You didn't see anything, did you? Neither did I."

The very blustery night had become stormy. Rain was falling outside the window, and the sky was full of lightning flashes and the rumble of thunder. Pooh kept his lonely vigil hour after hour, dragging his gun at his side until finally, overcome with sleepiness, he slid down beside the window and fell fast asleep. Fell fast asleep and began to dream.

Pooh's Dream

An army of honey pots marched toward him chanting a fearsome song about Heffalumps and Woozles that were coming after Pooh Bear in a threatening sort of way.

The honey pots appeared and vanished, marched toward him and marched away from him, and finally pursued Pooh, who tried to outrun them while looking back over his shoulder.

He ran right into a Heffalump and then into a Woozle and then he was surrounded by all kinds of strange creatures who started out as one thing and ended up as something entirely different. In his dream Pooh was chased by a Heffalump that looked like a bumblebee and it stole his honey jar. While Pooh was running away, he stumbled over some blocks that spelled H·U·N·N·Y and they turned into jack-in-the-boxes that laughed horrible laughs at him.

Finally Pooh was surrounded by all kinds of wild creatures, all after his new jar of honey. And suddenly there were some large balloons up in the sky where flashes of lightning appeared. The balloons poured water down, lots and lots of water, and Pooh grabbed an umbrella and was floating in the water while he heard the honey pots singing, *"Beware, beware, beware."*

He woke with a start to find himself sitting on the floor in his own house, in a deep puddle of water.

It was raining so hard that Pooh's house was flooded. As a matter of fact, it was raining all over the Hundred Acre Wood, and *everything* was flooded.

It rained and it rained and it rained. The water was rising round Piglet's tree, and Piglet thought to himself that he had never in his whole life seen so much rain. And he was what—three or four years old?

The rain came raining down in rushing rivulets till the river crept out of its bed and crept right into Piglet's. Piglet sat up in his big lonely bed and watched the water rise around it. He was frightened.

"If only," he thought, "Pooh, or Christopher Robin, or Rabbit were with me so we could tell each other how awful this is." It would have been jolly to share the excitement.

Then Piglet remembered a story he'd heard about a man on a desert island who had written a message, put it in a bottle, and floated it off to sea.

Piglet found a piece of paper and wrote a message:

HELP!
PIGLET (ME)

He found a bottle with a cork and put the message in it and threw the bottle out the window. He watched it bob and float in the water until it disappeared from sight. "I hope somebody finds it and then finds me," he thought. "I wish Pooh were here. It's so much cozier with two."

Meanwhile, Pooh had had to leave his flooded house. He had climbed out on a high limb of his tree, safe above the flood, and then decided he had better rescue his supper as well. One by one he brought his ten honey pots out and set them on the branch beside him. Then he was ready to have a little snack. He stuck his head in a pot, lost his balance, and toppled into the river below.

There was Pooh, upside down in the water with his head stuck in the pot. He was able to float very well in his honey-pot canoe, but he couldn't see a thing. The water twirled and tossed him while the rain came down and the Hundred Acre Wood got floodier and floodier.

But the water couldn't come up to Christopher Robin's house on high ground. And that's where everyone was gathering. Tigger, Rabbit, Kanga, and Roo paddled there in upside-down umbrellas. It was a time of great excitement.

Eeyore floated over on a door that made a kind of raft, and in the

midst of all this commotion he stuck stubbornly to his task of house-hunting for Owl.

Meanwhile, little Roo, playing at the water's edge, made an important discovery. "Look!" he called. "I've rescued a bottle and it's got something in it, too!"

He brought it to Christopher Robin, who knew how to read. Christopher removed the piece of paper and examined it carefully. "It's a message and it says: 'HELP! PIGLET (ME).'"

Christopher looked up at Owl, who was sitting on the limb of a tree. "Owl," he said, "you fly over to Piglet's house and tell him we'll make a rescue."

So Owl flew out over the flood and there was Piglet, floating on a chair, and there was Pooh bobbling along with his head stuck in a honey pot.

When Piglet saw Owl he cried out, "I don't mean to complain, but, oh, Owl, I'm s-s-scared."

"Now, now, be brave, little Piglet," said Owl, who perched on Pooh and his honey pot. "A rescue is being planned."

"It's awfully hard to be brave when you're such a s-s-small animal," Piglet stammered.

"Then to divert your small mind," Owl said kindly, "from your unfortunate predicament, I shall tell you a story about a distant cousin of mine." And he settled himself more comfortably on upside-down Pooh and began his tale.

Meanwhile, Piglet's floating chair was turning in circles in the water and there was the sound of rushing rapids. Interrupting Owl's story, Piglet cried out, "We're coming to a flutterfall, a flotterfill, a wa—a very big waterfall!"

"Please, no interruptions," said Owl, holding up his wing.

But it was too late. Piglet's chair went over the waterfall, and Pooh and Owl were swept over the falls, too. Owl simply flapped his wings and hovered above the water. Pooh's honey pot fell off of Pooh's head and onto Piglet, knocking him off his chair. In the tumbling waterfall Pooh went under for a second and came up seated on Piglet's chair. Owl, grateful for a perch, landed on the back of the chair as it floated down the river.

"Oh, there you are, Pooh Bear," he said. "Now, to continue my story . . ."

But at that moment the river carried them close to Christopher Robin's island, and Christopher, who had been on the lookout for his friends, called, "Look! There's Pooh! Over here, Pooh!"

The chair floated right up to the island.

"Pooh!" cried Christopher Robin.

"Oh, hello!" said Pooh, and they rushed into each other's arms.

"Thank goodness you're safe!" said Christopher Robin. "But have you seen Piglet?"

At that the honey pot bobbed up from under the chair and Piglet stuck his head out. "Here I am."

Christopher turned to his Bear. "Pooh," he said, "you rescued Piglet."

"I did?" Pooh asked.

"Yes, and it was a very brave thing to do."

"It was?"

"You are a hero," Christopher said.

"I am?" said Pooh looking modestly down his nose.

"Yes," Christopher said, "and as soon as the flood's over I shall give you a hero party."

Some days later the flood was over, the sun was shining, and the ground was back where it belonged, high and dry. A party table with a fresh white cloth and good things to eat, with party hats and favors for everyone, was set up in front of Christopher Robin's house.

Christopher Robin, at the head of the table, stood up and banged his spoon on a plate. "Attention, everybody," he said. "Now, this party is a hero party because of what someone did, and that someone is . . ."

Eeyore cleared his throat. "I found it," he announced.

"Found what, Eeyore?" Christopher asked.

"House for Owl."

Owl flapped his wings. "I say, Eeyore, good show."

"Oh, isn't it wonderful? Uh, where is it, Eeyore?" asked Piglet.

"If you want to follow me, I'll show it to you," said the gray donkey.

So everyone followed Eeyore. Then, to the surprise of all, Eeyore stopped right in front of Piglet's house with the TRESPASSERS WILL sign in front.

"Why are you stopping here, Eeyore?" Christopher asked.

"This is it. Owl's new house."

"Oh, dear, mercy me," said Piglet.

Eeyore continued, "Name's on it and everything," and he pointed proudly to the sign on which Owl had just landed.

"W-O-L, that spells OWL," Eeyore said proudly.

"Bless my soul, so it does," replied Owl.

"Well, Christopher, what do you think of it?" Eeyore asked.

"It's a nice house, Eeyore, but . . ."

"It's a lovely house, Eeyore, but . . ." added Kanga.

And Piglet sobbed, "It's the best house in the whole world!"

Pooh whispered, "Tell them it's your house, Piglet."

"No, Pooh." Piglet gulped, and then he said loud and clear, "This house belongs to our very good friend, Owl."

"But Piglet," Rabbit said in a worried voice. "Where will you live?"

Piglet had begun to sob again.

"Well, I guess I shall live . . . I suppose I shall live . . ."

Pooh reached over and took Piglet's hand. "With me. You shall live with me. Won't you, Piglet?"

Piglet wiped his eyes with his free hand. "With you?" he asked between sniffs. "Oh, thank you, Pooh Bear. Of course I will."

Christopher Robin leaned down. "Piglet, that was a very grand thing to do."

"A heroic thing to do," Rabbit added.

Pooh had an idea. "Christopher Robin, can you make a one-hero party into a two-hero party?"

"Of course we can, silly old Bear," said Christopher Robin.

And so Pooh was a hero for saving Piglet, and Piglet was a hero for giving Owl his beloved home in the beech tree. All the animals marched back to the party table, with Owl leading the way, Christopher Robin beating his drum, Kanga hopping, with Roo jouncing in her pouch, Tigger doing his bouncy dance, Piglet atop Pooh, and Pooh atop Eeyore, with Rabbit bringing up the rear.

"Hip-hip-Pooh-ray, hip-hip-Pooh-ray for Winnie the Pooh!" they all shouted.

"And Piglet, too," Piglet added in a happy squeak.

WINNIE THE POOH AND TIGGER TOO

On a lovely sunny morning Winnie the Pooh, who was a Bear of Very Little Brain, was sitting in his Thoughtful Spot trying hard to think of something to do and someone to do it with. And while he was thinking, all of a sudden he was flat on his back with Tigger bouncing on top of him.

"Oh, hello, Pooh. Rrrrrrr," growled Tigger. "I'm Tigger. T-I-double grrr. That spells Tigger."

"Yes, I know," said Pooh. "You've bounced me before."

"Well, well," Tigger laughed, leaning down on Pooh's nose. "I remember you. You're the one that's stuffed with fluff. Well, I gotta go now. I have a lot of bouncing to do. Whooo! TTFN! That's 'Ta-ta for now!'" And away Tigger bounced down the road, while Pooh brushed himself off and went back to thinking his thoughts.

Piglet was out in front of the house sweeping the path, when suddenly he was rolling on it with a large animal bouncing on top of him.

"Rrrrrrr. Hello, Piglet. I'm Tigger."

"Oh, Tigger!" Piglet gasped. "You s-s-s-scared me!"

"Shucks," laughed Tigger. "That was just one of my *little* bounces."

"It was?" Piglet asked in a shaky voice. "Oh, thank you, Tigger."

"Yeah," said Tigger. "I'm saving my best bounce for Old Long Ears," and he pulled his own ears up like a rabbit's.

Piglet sat up and watched Tigger bounce off down the path. "Ta-ta," Tigger called over his shoulder, but Piglet didn't get to his feet until Tigger had bounced safely out of sight.

Rabbit was out in his vegetable garden gathering vegetables and humming a contented little song. "There," he said as he picked a bunch of carrots. "That should do it," and he looked proudly at his wheelbarrow full of fresh vegetables.

Suddenly he saw Tigger bouncing along in his direction.

"Oh, no!" Rabbit cried out.

Tigger, with one big bounce, bowled over Rabbit and his wheelbarrow, knocking vegetables left and right.

"Hello, Rabbit!" he called cheerily, standing on Rabbit's chest. "I'm Tigger. T-I-double grrr."

"Oh, please," Rabbit groaned. "Please don't spell it." He looked around at his scattered vegetables. "Oh, dear. Just see what you've done to my beautiful garden!"

"Yuck," said Tigger who had stuck his foot into a ripe pumpkin. "Messy, isn't it?"

Rabbit was hopping mad. "Messy? Messy?" he shouted. "It's ruined. Ruined, that's what it is, Tigger." He glared at Tigger. "Oh, why don't you ever stop bouncing?" he scolded.

"Why?" Tigger was amazed. "That's what Tiggers do best! Whooo!" And he danced back and forth in front of Rabbit singing his bouncy song.

The very next day Rabbit decided something had to be done. He called a protest meeting about Tigger at his house, and he and Pooh and Piglet sat down together to figure out what to do to keep Tigger from bouncing on them.

Rabbit knocked on the table for order. "Order, please. Now, I say Tigger's getting too bouncy nowadays. It is time we taught him a lesson."

Pooh and Piglet nodded their heads.

"No matter how much we like him," Rabbit continued, "you can't deny, he bounces just too much."

Piglet, the smallest of the group, spoke up timidly. "Oh, excuse me, Rabbit, but perhaps if we could think of a way of unbouncing Tigger, uh, it would be a very good idea, huh?"

"Exactly, Piglet," said Rabbit. "Just what I feel." And Piglet turned bright pink with pleasure.

"Ah, what do you feel?" Rabbit turned to Pooh. "Pooh?" he asked. But Pooh was snoozing. Piglet jabbed Pooh. "Haven't you been listening to Rabbit?" he asked.

"I listened," Pooh explained sleepily, "but then, I had a small piece of fluff in my ear. Could you say it again, please, Rabbit?"

"Well, where should I start from?" Rabbit asked patiently.

Pooh thought a bit. "From the moment the fluff got in my ear," he answered.

"And when was that?" Rabbit asked, still patient.

"I don't know," Pooh replied. "I couldn't hear properly."

Piglet whispered into Pooh's ear, "We were just trying to think of a way to get the bounce out of Tigger," he explained.

"Ah," Pooh nodded. Now he understood.

But meanwhile Rabbit had had a splendid idea. "Now listen," he said, quite excited. "We'll take Tigger for a long explore, see? Someplace where he's never been." Rabbit was pacing back and forth quite pleased. "And we'll lose him there!" he laughed.

"Lose him?" Pooh asked. "Why?"

"Oh, we'll find him again. Next morning," Rabbit answered. "And mark my words, he'll be a humble Tigger. A small and sad Tigger. And an 'oh-Rabbit-am-I-glad-to-see-you' Tigger. And it'll take the bounce out of him. That's why."

"Now," said Rabbit, holding up his hand. "All in favor say 'aye.'"

Piglet raised his hand and jabbed Pooh, who had nodded off again.

"Aye," said Piglet. "Pooh! Pooh!"

Pooh woke with a start. "Ah, here!" he called out hastily.

"Good," laughed Rabbit. "That's good. Motion carried."

So it was agreed that the three friends and their new friend Tigger would start on their long explore the very next morning. The weather turned out cold and misty. The woods were gray and it was not easy to see where you were going—or where you had been.

Rabbit, Piglet, and Pooh (who, as usual, had brought along a little something to sustain himself) walked together while Tigger bounced, now ahead, now behind, further and further into the mist. Finally, Rabbit thought it was a good time to follow their plan and lose Tigger, who had bounced quite out of sight. They had come to a hollow log.

"Now's our chance," Rabbit whispered. "QUICK!" and he ran into the log with Pooh and Piglet following. "In here. Hide!"

Huddled together inside the dark log, they were very quiet for a long time—maybe two minutes. "Tigger's lost now, isn't he, Rabbit?" whispered Piglet.

"Oh, he's lost all right, Piglet," Rabbit answered.

Piglet laughed. "Oh, goody! This is lots of fun, Pooh, isn't it?"

Rabbit peered out of his end of the log. No Tigger in sight.

"My splendid idea worked," he reported. "Now, home we go!"

"Yum, yum, it's time for lunch," Pooh said happily, starting to climb over Rabbit to get out of the log.

But suddenly, there was Tigger's voice—"Hello!"—and Rabbit pulled Pooh back into the log. "Oh, my goodness. Hide!" he whispered.

Tigger was bouncing on and off the log, yelling, "Hello! Hey, you blokes, where are you?" His tail got caught in a crack of the log and Tigger pulled and pulled to get it free. "Hey, where the heck are you guys?" he hollered, pulling at his tail. Rabbit and Pooh, inside the log, quietly helped free the tail and Tigger, with a great yell, fell over backwards.

"HELLOOOO!" he shouted as he bounced off of the log and away into the woods. "Rabbit, Piglet, Pooh, where are you?" he called, his voice growing fainter and fainter as he went further into the woods. "HELLOOOO!"

Rabbit peered out of the log, then he and the others crawled out.

"Hooray, we've done it!" he laughed. "Now, come on, hurry. Let's head for home."

Well, Rabbit was certain that his plan had worked, and so it seemed at first. But after a while, he and Pooh and Piglet had been walking for a long long time and they kept seeing the same old sand pit.

"It's a funny thing how everything looks the same in the mist," said Rabbit.

"He's right, Piglet. It's the very same sand pit," said Pooh.

"Well, it's lucky I know the forest so well or . . . or . . . or we might get lost," Rabbit told them. "Come on, follow me."

Now Pooh was getting tired of seeing the same old sand pit. And he was beginning to suspect it of following them about. No matter which direction they started in, they always seemed to end up at it.

"Uh, Rabbit?" Pooh asked.

"Yes?"

"Say, Rabbit, how would it be if as soon as we're out of this old pit, we just try to find it again?"

"What's the good of that?"

"Well," Pooh explained. "We keep looking for home, but we keep finding this pit. So I just thought that if we looked for *this*, we might find home."

Rabbit scratched his ear. "I don't see much sense in that, Pooh. If I walked away from this pit and then walked back to it, of course I should find it. I'll prove it to you." And Rabbit walked off into the mist.

Pooh and Piglet waited near the sand pit for Rabbit. They waited, and waited, and waited. And all the while Pooh's thoughts kept returning

to his honey pots at home. Finally, he and Piglet sat down and rested in the sand pit and pretty soon they fell asleep, Piglet with his head on Pooh's stomach.

Something growled, and Piglet jumped up: "What . . . wh . . . what was that, Pooh?"

Pooh sat up. "My tummy rumbled because I'm so hungry. Now then, come on, Piglet. Let's go home."

Pooh and Piglet climbed out of the sand pit.

"But, Pooh, do you know the way?" Piglet asked, peering into the mist.

"No, Piglet. But there are twelve pots of honey in my cupboard. And they have been calling to my tummy."

"They have?" Piglet tried to listen, too.

"Yes, Piglet. I couldn't hear them before because Rabbit would talk so. But I think I know where they're calling from. So come on. We'll just follow my tummy."

So the two of them walked off together into the misty woods. And for a long time Piglet said nothing, so as not to interrupt Pooh's honey pots.

And sure enough, as the mist got thinner, and just when Piglet began to know where he was . . . something knocked them flat on the ground and stood on them.

"Hello, you two blokes. Where have you been?" Tigger laughed his bounciest laugh.

Pooh and Piglet got up and dusted themselves off. "We've been trying to find our way home," said Pooh.

"Pooh," Piglet whispered, "I don't think Rabbit's splendid idea worked."

"Say, where is Old Long Ears, anyway?" asked Tigger.

"He must still be missing in the mist," Pooh told him.

"Well," Tigger laughed. "Leave it to me. I'll bounce him right out of there." And he rushed past Pooh and Piglet, bouncing merrily down the path. "TTFN!" he called. "Ta-ta for now."

In another part of the woods, Rabbit was still wandering around in the mist. By now he was quite lost and bewildered, and to make matters worse, his mind was beginning to play tricks on him. Every rock seemed to be a monster, the splash of frogs jumping into the pond startled him, their croaking noises scared him out of his wits. Rabbit started to run, in a panic. And ran right into something that bounced on top of him.

"Tigger!" Rabbit yelled. "But you're supposed to be lost!"

Tigger, looking down at Rabbit, said, "Oh, Tiggers never get lost, Bunny Boy," and he patted Rabbit's face.

"Never . . . get . . . lost!" Rabbit repeated as best he could with a Tigger on his chest. "Oh, no!"

"Come on, Rabbit," said Tigger, helping Rabbit up. "Let's go

home. Hang on! Whoo!" And off he bounced with Rabbit holding onto his tail for dear life.

So they headed back and Rabbit was now a humiliated Rabbit, a lost-and-found Rabbit, and a why-oh-why-do-these-things-happen-to-me Rabbit. But Tigger was as bouncy as ever.

It was winter and the first snowfall covered the Hundred Acre Wood. Kanga was out sweeping the snow off of her front walk while Roo waited on top of the mailbox, looking out for Tigger, who had promised to take him for a romp. Suddenly there was a whoosh of snow, knocking Roo off the mailbox.

"Well, here I am," Tigger called as he slid up to Roo. "Did I surprise you, Roo?"

"I like surprises," Roo smiled at his big friend.

"Are you ready for some bouncing?"

Roo nodded happily. "Yeah! You and I are good bouncers, aren't we?" He was in a dither of impatience to be off with Tigger.

But Kanga unwound her warm muffler. "Just a moment, dear," she said firmly, looping it around Roo's neck while he practiced his bounces. "Hold still. My, but you're bouncy today!"

Roo did a few more bounces. "That's what Roos do the bestest."

"All right, now keep your scarf on," Kanga said anxiously as she watched Roo and Tigger bounce off in the snow. "And Tigger, have Roo home in time for his nap, and be careful," she called after them.

"Don't worry, Mrs. Kanga. I'll take care of the little fellow. Whoo!"

The pond was frozen smooth as glass and Rabbit was skating on it in long graceful swoops, enjoying the perfect winter day. "Peace and quiet," he sighed. "And thank goodness, no Tigger."

Just then, at the other end of the pond Tigger and Roo bounced to the edge of the ice. "Hey, look!" Tigger said. "If it isn't Old Long Ears."

Roo watched Rabbit gliding smoothly into a figure eight. "Can Tigger ice-skate as fancy as Mr. Rabbit?" he asked.

Tigger puffed out his chest. "Can Tiggers ice-skate? Why that's what Tiggers do best." And he slid onto the ice with a whoop and a holler. "Hey, this is a cinch!" he yelled. "Wheee!" He spun on his tail—and suddenly went quite out of control.

Rabbit watched Tigger spinning toward him. "Oh, no!" he groaned. "Not him!"

"Look out," Tigger called, sliding wildly across the ice. "Oh! Oh! I can't . . . Look out!"

Rabbit scrambled out of the way, but Tigger was slipping and twirling off balance. "Out of the way!" he shouted. "Look out!"

But it was no use. He spun into Rabbit and then burrowed into a snowbank. Rabbit was knocked clear across the ice and through the front door of his house. Looking about at all of his furniture knocked down, his dishes scattered, his lamps and books fallen on the floor, poor Rabbit could only hold his aching head in his hands and moan, "Why does it always have to be me? Why, oh why, oh why?"

Outside, Roo bounced onto the mound of snow where Tigger was buried. "Tigger, Tigger, are you all right?"

Tigger rose slowly from the snow, brushing himself off.

"Yuck," he said. "Tiggers don't like ice-skating."

So Tigger and Roo went farther into the Hundred Acre Wood looking for something that Tiggers do best. Roo gazed up at the tall trees with their bare winter branches.

"I'll bet you could climb trees, huh, Tigger?"

"Climb trees? Whooo, that's what Tiggers do best." And Tigger waited while Roo bounced onto his shoulders. "Only Tiggers don't *climb* trees. They *bounce* them. Come on, let's go!"

So there went Tigger, with Roo on his shoulders, bouncing up to the lowest limb of a very tall tree. "Whooooo!" he shouted, bouncing from limb to limb. "Whoops!" he yelled as a particularly high bounce made him grab onto the tree trunk. Roo was bounced off his shoulder and fell, grabbing Tigger's tail on the way down.

"I almost bounced you clear out of the tree!" Tigger apologized, looking down at Roo. "Say, how did this tree get so high?" Tigger clutched at the slender trunk near the top of the tree. It began to sway. "Hey! Hey! Hey! What's happening now?" he asked, beginning to feel a little dizzy.

But Roo was having a wonderful time swinging on Tigger's tail and singing:

> *Don't swing on a string,*
> *It's much too frail.*
> *The best part to swing*
> *Is a Tigger's tail. Wheee!*

Tigger held on to the tree as he swayed back and forth with Roo's energetic swinging.

"S . . . S . . . Stop that, kid," he moaned. "Please stop. You're rocking the forest."

Roo looked up at his friend, who seemed to be feeling sick. He let go of Tigger's tail and landed on a branch below.

"What's the matter, Tigger?"

Tigger held tight to the tree. "Whew!" he exclaimed. "Thank goodness! I was just getting seasick from swaying too much."

While Tigger and Roo were having their adventure in the tree-tops, Pooh and Piglet were having problems of their own. Pooh was walking around a tree, carefully staring at the ground. Piglet watched for a minute. "What are you doing, Pooh?"

"Shhh," whispered Pooh. "Tracking something."

"Tracking what?"

"Well, that's just what I asked myself, Piglet. What?"

Pooh walked about with his eyes fixed on the ground while Piglet scurried after him. "And what do you think you'll answer yourself?"

"I shall have to wait until I catch up with it," Pooh replied.

Piglet looked at his friend admiringly. "Pooh," he said at last. "For a Bear of Very Little Brain, you sure are a smart one."

"Thank you, Piglet."

Pooh pointed to the snowy ground in front of him. "What do you see here, Piglet?" he asked.

"Tracks," Piglet answered. "Paw marks." He moved closer to Pooh and said in a squeaky voice, "Oh, Pooh, do you think it could be a, a . . . Woozle?"

"Maybe," said Pooh. "Sometimes it is and sometimes it isn't. You never can tell with paw marks."

Suddenly Pooh stopped and bent over the tracks.

"Ah-ha!" he exclaimed.

Piglet started and grabbed Pooh's arm.

"Ah-ha what?" he stammered.

Pooh bent over and looked at the snow now thickly marked with footprints.

"A very mysterious thing, Piglet. A whole new set of tracks, see?"

And so it seemed to be. There were the tracks, joining each other here and getting mixed up with each other there. But to Pooh, quite plainly, two different sets of paw marks.

"Piglet, whatever it was that made these tracks has now been joined by another whatever-it-is and both of them are now proceeding in company."

"I wasn't exactly expecting company," said Piglet anxiously.

"Neither was I," Pooh admitted. "Would you mind coming with me, Piglet, just in case they turn out to be Animals of Hostile Intent?"

Piglet said he had nothing to do until Friday anyway, and would be delighted to join Pooh—in case it really *was* a Woozle, or even two Woozles.

Just then they heard a loud cry, "HELLLOOOO!"

Piglet and Pooh jumped with fright and clutched at each other.

Looking around and down and up Pooh pointed to something near the top of a tall tree.

"Look, Piglet! There's something way up in the tree . . . over there!"

Piglet moved still closer to Pooh. "Is it one of the Fiercer Animals?" he asked in a trembling voice.

Just then the cry came again, "HELLLOOOO!"

Piglet jumped up into Pooh's arms.

"It's a jagular," Pooh said in a trembly voice.

"What do jagulars do, Pooh?"

"Well," said Pooh, setting Piglet down, "jagulars always call 'Hellloooo' and then when you look up, they drop on you."

Piglet stared hard at the ground. "I'm looking down, Pooh," he said.

Again the cry came, "HELLLOOOO!"

And high up in the tree Roo said, "Hey, Tigger, it's Pooh and Piglet down there." And he yelled in his squeaky voice, "Pooh! Piglet!"

Looking up, Pooh could now see who it was in the treetop. "Why it's only Roo and Tigger," he said to Piglet. "Come on."

So Pooh and Piglet walked over and stood at the bottom of the tall tree.

"Hello, Roo," Pooh called. "Hey, what are you and Tigger doing way up there?"

Roo was sitting comfortably on a branch, swinging his feet. "I'm all right but Tigger's stuck."

Indeed, Tigger was clinging to the tree with a very worried look on his face.

"Help, somebody, please," he wailed. "Get Christopher Robin!"

Well, it wasn't too long before word got back to Christopher Robin and the others that Tigger was in trouble, and they rushed right over.

"Hello, Pooh. Hello, Piglet," said Christopher. "What's up?"

"Tigger and Roo are up." Pooh pointed to the top of the tree.

"Oh, my goodness!" Kanga exclaimed. "Roo, how did you get way up there?"

Roo, swinging gaily on his branch, yelled down, "Easy, Mama, we bounced up."

"Gracious!" Kanga watched nervously. "Do be careful, dear."

"I'm all right, Mama, but Tigger's stuck!"

"Oh, what a shame," said Kanga. "That's too bad."

"Wrong!" Rabbit spoke up. "That's *good*. You see, he can't bounce anybody up there."

Meanwhile, Christopher Robin was taking off his coat. "Oh, dear. We'll just have to get him down, somehow," he said.

Rabbit was disappointed. "Down? Down?" he demanded. "Do we have to?"

But Christopher paid no attention. He gave everyone a corner of his coat to hold so it made a kind of safety net. Then he called up to Roo. "You're first, Roo. Jump!"

Kanga said fearfully. "Try not to fall too fast, dear." But Roo thought it was a great lark. "Wheeeee!" he yelled as he sailed down, bounced once on Christopher Robin's coat and straight into Kanga's arms.

"Oh, thank goodness." Kanga held Roo tight and gave him a big kiss.

Roo called up to Tigger, "Come on, Tigger. It's fun. It doesn't hurt. Jump!"

But Tigger still held dizzily to the tree.

"Jump!" Christopher Robin yelled.

"Jump?" Tigger demanded. "Tiggers don't jump. They bounce."

"Well, then," said Pooh helpfully. "Bounce down."

"Oh, don't be ricky–diculus, Pooh," said Tigger, clinging to the tree. "Tiggers only bounce *up*!"

"Then climb down, Tigger," Christopher suggested.

But Tigger was afraid to move. "Tiggers can't climb down, Christopher Robin, uh, because, ah, because, ah, ah, their tail gets in the way."

Rabbit jumped up and down for joy. "Hooray, that settles it!" he shouted. "If he won't jump and he can't climb down, then we'll just have to leave him up there forever!"

Tigger didn't like that idea at all. "Forever? Oh, if I ever get out of this I promise never to bounce again. Never."

Rabbit did a happy hop. "Did you hear him promise?" he shouted. "He promised not to bounce any more. Did you hear him, everybody?"

"Come along," Christopher called to Tigger. "You can let go now. We'll catch you in my coat."

"Just wait a minute," said Tigger nervously, and then he put his paws over his eyes and went. "Ooh, ooh!" he yelled, and the next thing he knew he had landed in a soft pile of snow.

"Good old terra firma!" he said, scooping up heaps of the snow and kissing it for joy.

"I'm so happy to be back on the ground. I feel like bouncing!" Tigger exclaimed, as he bounced around a bit.

Rabbit shook his head. "Remember, you promised."

Tigger sat down in the snow, looking very sad. "You mean I can't ever bounce again?" he asked.

"Never," Rabbit told him.

"Never? Not even just one teensy-weensy bounce?"

"Not even a smidgen of a bounce," Rabbit said sternly.

Tigger walked away sadly, his head and tail hanging down. He was not the lively old Tigger they all remembered.

Kanga, watching him, sighed, "Oh, the poor dear. That is too bad." And Roo felt terribly sorry for his friend. He pulled at Christopher Robin's coat and stood on tiptoe to whisper to him, "Christopher Robin, I like the old bouncy Tigger best."

"So do I, Roo. So do I."

Then Piglet spoke up, "I do too."

And Kanga said, "Of course, we all do. Don't you agree, Rabbit?"

"Well, ah . . . I ah . . . that is, ah . . . ah . . . what I mean . . ." Rabbit stammered.

"Well?" Pooh asked.

"Well, ah, all right," Rabbit said at last. "I ah . . . oh, all right. I guess I like the old Tigger better, too."

Upon hearing that, Tigger came bouncing over to join the others. "Oh, boy!" he shouted and bounced right into Rabbit, knocking him over. Sitting on top of Rabbit, Tigger gave him a big hug.

"You mean, I can have my bounce back?" he asked happily. And he picked Rabbit up. "C'mon, Rabbit. Let's you and me bounce, okay?"

"Good heavens!" Rabbit exclaimed, quite taken by surprise. "Ah, me bounce?"

"Why, certainly," Tigger told him. "Look, you've got just the feet for bouncing."

Rabbit looked at his long foot. "I have?"

"Sure," Tigger told him. "Come on, try it. Bouncing makes you feel just grrrrreat!"

Rabbit did a little trial bounce. Not bad. Then he tried another and his face lighted up with a big smile. "Well, say, it does!" he exclaimed. "C'mon everybody. Let's all bounce!"

And Tigger and Piglet, Roo and Kanga, Christopher Robin, Pooh and Rabbit bounced around in the snow like anything. Tigger was right. It made them all feel grrrrreat.

WINNIE THE POOH AND A DAY FOR EEYORE

Now, the Hundred Acre Wood had many natural wonders but none was lovelier than the tiny stream running through the forest. This little stream had a very long way to go and by the time it reached the edge of the forest it had grown up so it was almost a river. Being grown up, it said to itself, "Slow down. There is no hurry. We shall get there some day."

Crossing the river at its most peaceful spot was a broad wooden bridge with wooden rails on either side of it. Winnie the Pooh could just get his chin on the bottom rail, if he wanted to, but it was more fun to lie down on the bridge with his head under the rail and watch the river slipping by beneath him.

It was a favorite place where Pooh would often wander, just to do nothing in particular and to think nothing in particular. But on one of these wanders, something took his mind off of nothing.

"Plop," a cone fell off of a fir tree and dropped right on Pooh's head. Pooh picked it up and examined it carefully. "This is a very good fir cone," he said, "and something ought to rhyme to it so I can make up a song. Let me think." And he walked along holding the cone and trying out the words to a song:

> *Now, fir cones belong in trees,*
> *High up with the buzzing bees,*
> *But this one I found*
> *Down on the ground,*
> *Freed by a gentle breeze.*

"Oops!" Pooh tripped over a tree root and tumbled down the little hill that led to the bridge. The fir cone fell with him, and when Pooh landed on his back on the bridge, the cone bounced once on his nose, then popped into the stream.

"Oh, bother," said Pooh, looking over the right side of the bridge and watching the stream below carry his fir cone away. "I suppose I shall have to find another one."

He had every intention of searching for another cone and finishing his song, but as he looked down at the river slipping away so peacefully beneath the bridge his thoughts began to slip away with it.

"That's funny," he said as he noticed his fir cone floating lazily under the bridge. "I dropped it on the other side and it came out on this side. I wonder if it would do it again?"

Pooh collected an armful of cones under the fir tree but by the time he returned to the bridge he had spilled all but two of them. He leaned over the railing and dropped his last two fir cones into the stream below. Then he crossed over to the other railing and peered down.

"I wonder which one will come out first," he thought.

Well, the big one came out first and the little one came out last, which was exactly what Pooh wanted. And that was the beginning of a wonderful new game called Pooh Sticks, which Pooh invented. He taught it to Christopher Robin and all his friends, and the reason it is called Pooh Sticks is because they play it now with sticks instead of fir cones, sticks being easier to mark with their names.

One day Pooh and Piglet and Rabbit and Roo were all on the bridge playing Pooh Sticks.

"All right," said Rabbit, holding his stick. "The first stick to pass all the way under the bridge wins. Go!" They all dropped their sticks into the stream and ran to the other side of the bridge, leaning over the edge to see whose stick would float by first.

"I can see mine!" cried Roo. "Can you see yours, Pooh?"

"No, I expect my stick's stuck."

"They always take longer than you think," Rabbit explained.

"Oh, I can see yours, Piglet," Pooh exclaimed.

"Mine's a sort of grayish one," said Piglet, who was careful not to lean over too far lest he fall in.

"Yes, that's what I see," Pooh said. "It's coming over to my side!"

Roo jumped up and down with excitement and Rabbit had to catch him. "Come on, stick!" he hollered. "Stick, stick, stick!"

Piglet was very excited, too, because his gray one was the first to be seen and that meant he was winning. "Are you sure it's mine?" he asked anxiously.

"Ooh," squeaked Roo. "It's a big gray one. Here it comes. A very big gray . . ."

"No, it isn't," Rabbit said. "It's Eeyore." And there, indeed, was Eeyore, the gray donkey, floating on his back, calm and dignified, with his legs up in the air.

"Don't pay any attention to me," said Eeyore as he passed beneath the bridge. "Nobody ever does."

"I didn't know you were playing," Roo exclaimed.

"I'm not," Eeyore said.

"Eeyore, what are you doing down there?" Rabbit asked.

"Give you three guesses," the donkey said as he spun slowly around in the current.

"Fishing?" asked Pooh.

"Wrong."

"Going for a sail?" asked Piglet.

"Wrong again."

"Waiting for somebody to help you out of the river?" Rabbit asked.

"Right. Give Rabbit time and he'll get the answer," said Eeyore.

Piglet, leaning as far over the edge of the bridge as he dared, called down, "Eeyore, what can we . . . I mean, how should we . . . do you think if we . . ."

Eeyore, revolving slowly in a little eddy, said, "Yes, little Piglet. One of those would be just the thing. Thank you."

Everyone thought for a moment and then Pooh said, "I've got an idea, but I don't suppose it's a very good one."

Eeyore tipped under the water then spat out a big mouthful, like a whale. "I don't suppose it is either," he answered.

"Go on, Pooh," said Rabbit. "Let's have it."

"Well, if we all threw stones and things into the river on one side of Eeyore, the stones would make waves and the waves would wash him to the other side."

"That's a very good idea and I'm glad we thought of it, Pooh," said Rabbit.

Pooh, looking very happy, stumped off to find the biggest stone he could carry. He rolled it onto the bridge and leaned over the side, holding it in his paws. Rabbit directed him back and forth. "Up, Pooh? Piglet, give Pooh a little more room. Get back a bit there, Roo. I think a little to the left, Pooh. No, no, to the right. Yes."

Pooh called down to Eeyore, "Could you stop turning around for a moment because it muddles me rather?"

"I like turning. Especially around."

Rabbit decided it was time for him to take charge.

"Ah, Eeyore, when I say 'Now' Pooh will drop the stone."

"Thank you very much, Rabbit, but I expect I shall know."

Piglet and Roo and Eeyore closed their eyes while Rabbit counted, "Ah, one, two, NOW!"

Pooh pushed the stone off the bridge. There was a loud "KER-PLASH!" and bubbles floating on the water but Eeyore had disappeared. The little group on the bridge watched anxiously, but even seeing Piglet's stick come out ahead of Rabbit's under the bridge didn't cheer them. Eeyore was nowhere to be seen.

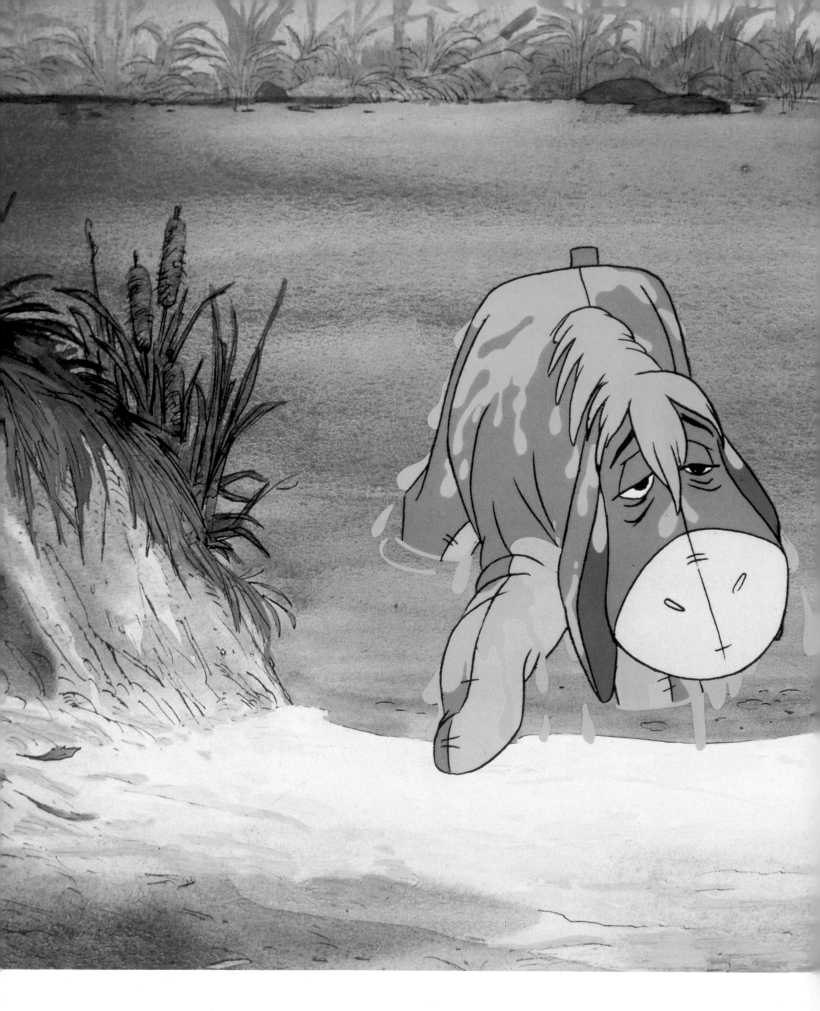

Pooh was thinking perhaps it hadn't been such a good idea after all when there, near the riverbank, was something gray.

"There he is!" called Roo. And they all watched the gray something grow bigger and bigger. And suddenly there was Eeyore, a very wet Eeyore, walking out of the water.

Everyone dashed off the bridge to join him on the riverbank.

"Oh, Eeyore," Piglet cried. "You are all wet!"

"That happens when you've been inside a river, little Piglet," Eeyore explained. "For quite a long time, at that."

"How did you fall in?" asked Rabbit.

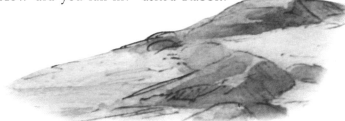

"I was BOUNCED," said Eeyore.

"Ooh, Eeyore," Roo squeaked. "Did somebody push you?"

"Somebody BOUNCED me," Eeyore complained. "I was thinking by the side of the river, minding my own business, when I received a loud BOUNCE."

"But who did it?" Pooh asked.

"I expect it was Tigger." Piglet looked around nervously.

"Eeyore," said Rabbit earnestly. "Was it . . . Tigger?" Just then there was a loud noise in the bushes and out bounced Tigger, tumbling Rabbit to the ground. "Hello, Rabbit," Tigger laughed. "Hello, everybody."

Rabbit brushed himself off and asked sternly, "Tigger, what happened just now?"

Tigger looked uncomfortable. "Just when?"

"When you bounced Eeyore into the river."

"I didn't bounce him," Tigger said.

"He bounced me," Eeyore insisted.

"Oh, I didn't really," Tigger explained. "I just had a cough and I

said, 'Grrrr-opp-ptschsch---grrrr---opp,' and I happened to be behind Eeyore."

Piglet put his hands over his ears, and Pooh said, "It's all right, Piglet," in a soothing sort of way.

"That's what I call bouncing," Eeyore insisted.

"Tigger, try bouncing me, Tigger," Roo demanded, jumping up and down.

"All I did was cough," Tigger insisted.

"You bounced," said Eeyore.

"Coughed."

"Bounced."

"Yeah, well, it was just a joke," Tigger confessed.

"Bouncy or coffy," Eeyore scolded, "it's all the same at the bottom of the river."

"Some people have no sense of humor," growled Tigger as he bounced off into the forest.

Rabbit looked after him and shook his head. "Tigger is so thoughtless with his bouncing," he sighed.

"Why should Tigger think of me?" said Eeyore sadly. "Nobody else does." And he walked slowly alongside the river until he and it reached his Gloomy Place.

Without a doubt something was troubling Eeyore, and his friends puzzled over what it might be.

The next day it rained, and Eeyore stood under a tree by the river in his Gloomy Place, which became even gloomier than usual. The gray donkey stood looking into the river while the rain fell on him. His sad face was reflected in the water.

"Pathetic," he said.

He turned and looked at his reflection from the other side. "Just as I thought," he sighed. "No better from this side."

There was a crackling noise in the bushes behind him and out walked Pooh. "Eeyore, what's the matter?" he asked.

"Nobody minds, nobody cares," said Eeyore. "Pathetic. That's what it is. What makes you think anything's the matter, Pooh Bear?"

"You seem so sad."

"Why should I be sad?" Eeyore asked, sitting down under a little rain cloud that rained on him. "It's my birthday. The happiest day of the year."

Pooh looked around at Eeyore's Gloomy Place. "Your birthday?" he asked. For there was no sign of a birthday celebration anywhere there.

"Of course," said the gray donkey. "Can't you see all the presents?"

"No," said Pooh.

"Can't you see the cake, the candles, and the pink sugar?"

"No," said Pooh again.

"Neither can I," Eeyore said. "Joke. Ha, ha!"

"Well," said Pooh. "Many happy returns of the day, Eeyore."

"Thank you, Pooh. But we can't all. And some of us don't."

"Can't all what?"

"No gaiety. No songs and dance. No 'Here we go 'round the mulberry bush.' But don't worry about me, Pooh. Go and enjoy yourself. I'll stay here and be miserable. With no presents. No cake. No candles." Eeyore was almost in tears.

It was too much for Pooh. "Wait right here!" he called to Eeyore

and he ran back home as fast as he could. He had to get poor Eeyore some sort of present and right away.

Who should Pooh find in front of his home but Piglet, who had climbed on a box and was jumping up and down in order to reach Pooh's door knocker.

"Piglet," he said. "What are you trying to do?"

"Reach the knocker. Hello, Pooh."

"Here, let me do it for you," said Pooh, knocking at the door.

"But Pooh, isn't this *your* house?"

"So it is," said Pooh. "Well, let's go in."

Once inside, Pooh explained to Piglet how this was poor Eeyore's birthday and nobody had taken any notice of it. "You know how gloomy Eeyore is anyhow. So I must get him a present of some sort."

Pooh looked around his house and his eyes lit on the honey pots in his cabinet. He had a quite small jar and he took it down. "This should do very well," he said. "What are you going to give, Piglet?"

"Couldn't I give it, too. From both of us?"

"No," Pooh shook his head. "That would not be a very good plan."

Piglet thought a bit. "Perhaps I could give Eeyore a balloon?"

"That," said Pooh, putting his arm around Piglet, "is a very good idea. Nobody could be uncheered by a balloon."

Piglet was quite excited. "I have one at home," he exclaimed. "I'll run home and get it right now."

So off Piglet trotted in one direction, and in the other direction went Pooh with his jar of honey. However, Pooh hadn't gone very far when a funny feeling began to creep over him. It started at the tip of his nose and trickled all the way down to the soles of his feet. As if someone inside him were saying, "Now then, Pooh. Time for a little something."

"Goodness," said Pooh. "I'd no idea it was so late. Good thing I brought this with me." And he sat down, opened the jar of honey, and had a little something. Then he had a little something more, and a little more, until he had taken the last lick from the inside of the jar.

"Now let me see," he said to himself as he got slowly to his feet. "Where was I going? Oh, yes. Eeyore! I was going to . . . oh, bother. I must give Eeyore *something*. But what?"

Well, maybe Owl could help. So Pooh headed for Owl's house in the Hundred Acre Wood first.

Owl had been hanging a picture when Pooh knocked at his door. "Good morning, Pooh," he said. "To what do I owe this . . ."

"Many happy returns of Eeyore's birthday, Owl."

"Oh, is that what it is? Well, come in, Pooh, come in."

"What are you giving him, Owl?"

"Giving who, Pooh?"

"Eeyore."

"Yes. I, uh . . . what are *you* giving him, Pooh?"

Pooh showed the pot to Owl. "I'm giving him this Useful Pot To Keep Things In," he said.

Owl took the pot and examined it. "Evidently someone has been keeping honey in it."

"You can keep *anything* in it," Pooh explained. "It's very useful like that. And I wanted to ask you . . ."

"You ought to write 'Happy Birthday' on it," Owl suggested.

"*That* was what I wanted to ask you. My spelling is wobbly."

Owl took the pot over to his table. He picked up a quill pen and

was about to start writing. "It's easier if people don't look while I'm writing," he said, waiting until Pooh moved back a bit. Then he started scratchily writing Pooh's message. It took a long time.

"It seems like a lot of words," said Pooh admiringly.

"Well, actually I wrote 'A Very Happy Birthday With Love From Pooh.' Naturally, it takes a good deal of words to say a long thing like that."

Pooh looked at his Useful Pot. It said: HIPY PAPY BTHUTHDTH THUTHDA BTHUTHDY.

"Eeyore will be most pleased, thank you, Owl." And Pooh hurried off to give his gift to Eeyore, while Owl flew directly to Christopher Robin's to tell him about Eeyore's birthday.

Meanwhile, Piglet was running along through the Hundred Acre Wood carrying a red balloon as big as he was when Owl flew overhead. "Many happy returns of Eeyore's birthday, Piglet!" he called. Piglet looked up and answered, "Many happy returns to you, too, Owl." And ran smack into a tree with his balloon.

There was a loud BANG!!??**!! Piglet lay face down on the ground holding his ears. Had the whole world blown up or only the Hundred Acre Wood, he wondered? Or was it only he, Piglet, and was he now alone on the moon and would he ever see Christopher Robin or Pooh or his other friends again?

He rolled over and opened his eyes. He was still in the Hundred Acre Wood. "Well, that's good," he thought, "but what could have made that terrible noise? And where is the balloon?" He looked at the ground next to him. "And what's this little piece of damp rag?"

Oh, dear, oh, dear, it was the balloon, the only balloon he had. Piglet picked up the little piece of damp rag and continued on his way. "Well, perhaps Eeyore doesn't *like* balloons so *very* much."

He trotted along sadly to Eeyore's Gloomy Place where he found Eeyore sitting under a tree, looking glum.

"Good afternoon, Eeyore," Piglet called.

"Good afternoon, little Piglet. If it is a good afternoon. Which I doubt."

"Many happy returns of the day," said Piglet.

Eeyore turned to stare at Piglet.

"Meaning my birthday?"

"Yes, Eeyore, and I . . . I've brought you a present."

"Pardon me, Piglet, but my hearing must be going." Eeyore raised his right hind leg carefully up to his ear. "Now, then, what were you saying?"

"I've brought you a present."

Eeyore put his right leg down, turned around, and raised his left hind leg to the other ear. "I thought you said you brought me a present."

"I did," said Piglet loudly. "I brought you a balloon."

"*Balloon?* Did you say balloon? One of those big round things you blow up?"

Piglet nodded. "Yes. But I'm afraid when I was running, that is, to bring it, I fell down and, ah . . ."

"Oh, dear," Eeyore was concerned. "You didn't hurt yourself, little Piglet?"

"No. But oh, Eeyore! I burst the balloon." And Piglet held out the little piece of damp rag. "Here it is, with many happy returns of the day."

"My balloon? My birthday balloon?"

Piglet nodded his head and began to sniffle.

Eeyore looked at what was left of his balloon.

"Red," he said. "My favorite color."

Piglet covered his eyes.

"If you don't mind my asking, Piglet, how big was it when it was a balloon?"

"About as big as m-m-m-me," Piglet stammered.

"Hmm. My favorite size."

Piglet and Eeyore stared sadly at what was left of the balloon. Piglet was too miserable to think of a thing to say. And then there was a shout from the riverbank and there was Pooh.

"Many happy returns of the day, Eeyore," he called, forgetting that he had said it earlier. He climbed the bank and set the honey pot down near Eeyore.

"I've brought you a little present, Eeyore. It's a Useful Pot. And it's got 'A Very Happy Birthday With Love From Pooh' written on it. And it's for putting things in. There!"

Eeyore looked at the pot and then he looked at his broken balloon. "Like a balloon!" he exclaimed to Pooh.

"Oh, no, Eeyore," Pooh explained. "Balloons are much too big to go into a pot . . ."

But Eeyore picked up the piece of balloon with his teeth and put it in the pot. Then he pulled it out and set it on the ground. And he picked it up again and carefully put it back in. "See," said Eeyore. "It goes in and out like anything."

"I'm very glad," said Pooh happily, "that I thought of giving you a Useful Pot To Put Things In."

"And I'm very glad," said Piglet happily, "that I thought of giving you Something To Put In A Useful Pot."

But Eeyore was smiling to himself and taking the balloon out and putting it back in.

Later that afternoon a beautiful birthday table was set up under the trees. Christopher Robin, Rabbit, Kanga and Roo, Pooh, Piglet, Owl, and Eeyore gathered round it. There was a cake with three pink candles and party hats and horns. And when the candles had been lit, Christopher Robin stood up and said, "Many happy returns, Eeyore."

And Eeyore took one mighty breath and blew out all three candles.

"Oh, bravo!" exclaimed Owl. "Bravo! Good show! This reminds me of the party we once gave for my Great-Uncle Robert." And while Christopher Robin cut slices of the cake and passed them around to everyone, Owl went on and on with the story about his Great-Uncle.

Just as Rabbit was handed his piece of cake, there was a loud "HALLOOO!"

Rabbit, all set to take a bite, groaned, "Oh, no. Oh, no, oh, no. Not Tigger!" And he went sprawling, with Tigger on top of him.

"Hello, Tigger," squeaked Roo. "We're having a party!"

Tigger sat up and laughed. "A party? Oh, boy, oh, boy. Tiggers *love* parties!" And he ran over to the table and grabbed a piece of birthday cake. "And cake!" he added, smacking his lips and licking frosting from his paws.

Rabbit followed Tigger to the table. "You've got a lot of nerve showing up here after what you did to Eeyore," he scolded.

Eeyore looked sad, remembering how he was bounced in the river.

Rabbit looked around the table at the others. "I think Tigger should leave," he said angrily.

Only Roo spoke up. "Aw, let him stay," he said, while Tigger nodded his head in agreement.

"What do you think, Christopher Robin?" Pooh asked.

Christopher Robin thought a moment. "I think we all ought to play Pooh Sticks," he decided.

"Pooh Sticks!" Tigger yelled, and he threw Rabbit around in some friendly roughhouse. "Boy, that's what Tiggers do best!"

So they all trooped over to the old wooden bridge and played the game for many contented hours, until the long afternoon came to an end. And Eeyore, who had never played Pooh Sticks before, won more times than anyone else.

But poor Tigger won none at all.

"Grrrr," said Tigger. "Tiggers don't like Pooh Sticks."

"Let's play again," begged Roo.

"We must go home now, dear," said Kanga firmly. "It's past your bedtime."

"Do we have to? I'm not tired," Roo begged as he followed his mother.

"Come along," she said.

"I think we should all be going," said Rabbit.

And Owl agreed. "Yes, quite right. Congratulations, Eeyore. It's been a delightful party."

"Thank you, Owl," Eeyore said, but he was watching Tigger sadly walk off into the forest, and he hurried to catch up with him.

"Tigger," he called. "I'd be happy to tell you my secret for winning at Pooh Sticks."

Tigger perked up. "You would?" he asked.

Eeyore and Tigger walked along together on a little path. "It's very easy," Eeyore explained. "You just have to let your stick drop in a twitchy sort of way."

"Oh, yeah. I forgot to twitch. That was my problem," and Tigger, full of confidence once more, gave a great bounce and landed right on Eeyore, knocking the gray donkey flat.

"Bounced again," Eeyore groaned.

In the last of the daylight Pooh and Piglet and Christopher Robin stood on the bridge, watching the river flow by beneath it.

"Tigger's all right, *really*," Piglet said at last.

"Of course he is," said Christopher Robin.

And Pooh added, "Everybody is, *really*. That's what I think. But I don't suppose I'm right."

"Of course you are right, silly old Bear," said Christopher Robin fondly.

THE END